TRANSFORMERS
EARTHSPARK

OPTIMUS PRIME AND MEGATRON'S
RACETRACK RECON!

By Ryder Windham

Illustrated by Patrick Spaziante

Simon Spotlight

New York   London   Toronto   Sydney   New Delhi

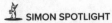 SIMON SPOTLIGHT

An imprint of Simon & Schuster Children's Publishing Division
1230 Avenue of the Americas, New York, New York 10020
This Simon Spotlight edition August 2023
TRANSFORMERS and all related characters are trademarks of Hasbro and are used with permission. TRANSFORMERS © 2023 Hasbro. All Rights Reserved. Transformers: EarthSpark TV series © 2023 Hasbro/Viacom International Inc. All Rights Reserved. Nickelodeon is a trademark of Viacom International Inc. All rights reserved, including the right of reproduction in whole or in part in any form. SIMON SPOTLIGHT and colophon are registered trademarks of Simon & Schuster, Inc. For information about special discounts for bulk purchases, please contact Simon & Schuster Special Sales at 1-866-506-1949 or business@simonandschuster.com.
Designed by Brittany Fetcho
The illustrations for this book were rendered digitally.
The text of this book was set in Proxima Nova.
Manufactured in the United States of America 0723 LAK
10 9 8 7 6 5 4 3 2 1
ISBN 978-1-6659-3787-0 (hc)
ISBN 978-1-6659-3786-3 (pbk)
ISBN 978-1-6659-3788-7 (ebook)

CONTENTS

CHAPTER 1
OFF TO THE RACES

"We have an important mission today. I need you to deploy for this one," said Special Agent Jon Schloder to Optimus Prime and Megatron. "You're going to the races!" Agent Schloder and the two Transformers robots were inside the Command Center in the secret underground headquarters of G.H.O.S.T., the Global Hazard and Ordinance Strike Team, located below the Witwicky Woods Ranger Station.

"Races?" wondered Optimus Prime. "Witwicky Racetrack does not have any races scheduled for today."

"You didn't let me finish," Agent Schloder said. "Today's races are outside town. Ever since the Transformers War ended fifteen years ago, I've been getting reports from around the world about yellow cars winning races. When G.H.O.S.T. went to those sites, we discovered traces of Energon. And you know what that means?"

Optimus Prime and Megatron looked at each other. "Does it mean yellow cars are faster than green cars?" asked Megatron with a hint of a smirk forming at his mouth.

"What?! No!" Schloder said. "It means Bumblebee is competing in these races! We still have not located him since the Transformers War ended. If Bumblebee enters today's race, I expect you two to find him. Any questions?"

"Just one," Megatron said. "Are you really, really sure yellow cars aren't faster than green cars?"

Schloder scowled.

"Megatron and I will go to the races at once, Agent Schloder," said Optimus Prime.

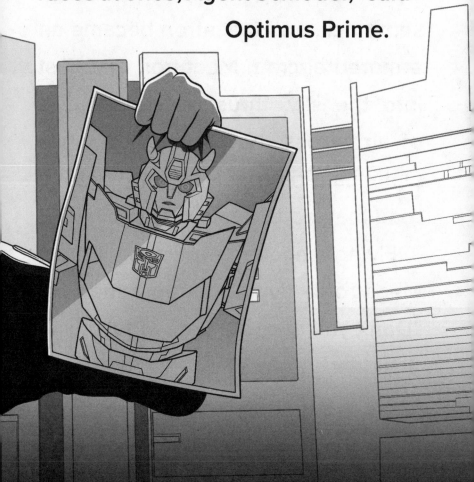

Leaving Agent Schloder in the Command Center, Optimus Prime and Megatron stepped outside to a parking lot next to the Ranger Station and changed into their alt modes. Optimus Prime became a large semitruck, and Megatron became an armored aircraft. Megatron rose fast into the sky, thrusting loud waves of air across the parking lot, while Optimus Prime roared out onto a road that led to a nearby highway.

Flying above Optimus Prime, Megatron activated his radio and said, "Don't you ever get tired of following Schloder's orders?"

Using his own radio, Optimus Prime responded, "We can't get tired of working with Schloder, old friend. When the Transformers War ended, you and I agreed to work with G.H.O.S.T. and help them ensure safe Cybertronian—Earth relations. Until we can guarantee that every Transformers robot can live in peace with humans, it is our duty to find and capture fugitive bots."

"But especially Decepticons," Megatron said with some bitterness. "After all, I don't know of any Autobots who have been locked up in G.H.O.S.T.'s underground prisons."

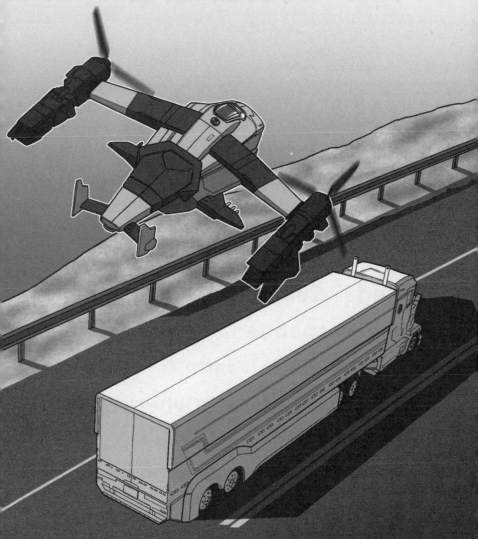

"We have to remain hopeful," Optimus Prime said, "that we can work with G.H.O.S.T. to eventually achieve freedom for all bots."

"And what if we find Bumblebee in a race today? Are you willing to bring our secret ally to Agent Schloder?" Megatron asked.

"We don't need to worry about seeing Bumblebee," Optimus Prime responded. "He's at the Malto family's farm, teaching the Terrans about Cybertronian history."

"Well, let's hope he doesn't find out there's a race anywhere near Witwicky," Megatron said, "because if there's one thing Bumblebee can't resist, it's any chance to test his speed!"

CHAPTER 2
GETTING UP TO SPEED

Bumblebee was in his alt mode as a sleek yellow sports car, driving fast in a tight circle and testing the grip of his tires on a broad patch of dirt at the Malto family's farm, when he remembered Optimus Prime's instructions.

"Uh-oh!" he said to himself as he skidded to a stop. "I'm late for class!"

Bumblebee changed into his bot mode and trotted over to the farm's big red barn, where the seven young Malto siblings were laughing and zooming around. Two of the siblings, Mo and her older brother,

Robby, were humans. The other five were known as the Terrans, the first Transformers robots born on Earth. The Terrans' names were Twitch, Thrash, Hashtag, Nightshade, and Jawbreaker.

The children were rapidly tossing and catching a football, a basketball, and a balloon at the same time. "All right, kids, settle down," Bumblebee said as he grabbed the basketball with one hand and accidentally popped the balloon with the other. "Time for a history lesson."

"But we're in the middle of a game!" Thrash said as he caught the football.

"Yeah," Twitch said, "and Robby and I were winning!"

"You can play later," Bumblebee said. "Optimus Prime wants me to teach you about how Transformers bots traveled from Cybertron to Earth, and—"

"I beg your pardon, Mr. Bumblebee," Nightshade said, "but you have already enlightened us with that particular tale."

"Oh," Bumblebee said. "Then I'll tell you about how Megatron quit the Decepticons so he could join forces with Optimus Prime and—"

"You told us that one, too," Mo said.

Before Bumblebee could suggest another option, Jawbreaker said, "Bumblebee, when you were young on Cybertron, what kinds of games did you play?"

"Mostly racing games," Bumblebee said. "There was a speedway where I used to—"

"A speedway?" Hashtag said with excitement. "Bumblebee, you just reminded me of something I saw in the news!" Hashtag extended the built-in satellite dish from her shoulder and held out her tablet. News items flashed across the tablet's screen before stopping at a headline: AMATEUR CAR AND MOTORCYCLE RACES TODAY. FREE ADMISSION.

Because Thrash's alt mode was a motorcycle with a sidecar, his eyes went wide as he heard the headline. "You and I should enter the races, Bumblebee!" he said.

"No way," Bumblebee replied. "What would your parents say?"

"But they're not even home! You're in charge," Robby said. "Mom told me she took the day off from work so she and Dad could go to the Witwicky Botanical Gardens!"

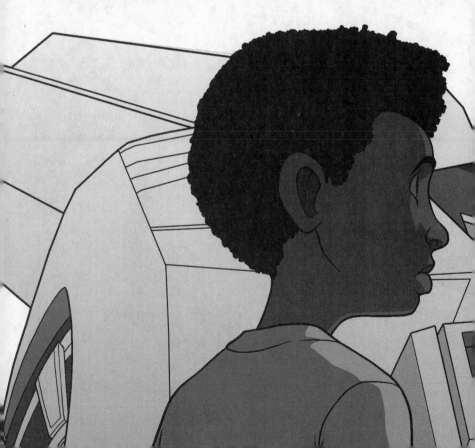

"Hmm," Bumblebee said. "I guess they'll never know if we sneak over to the speedway, but just to *watch* the races."

"Hooray!" Hashtag hollered. She changed into her alt mode as a large news van. "We're going on a field trip!"

Since Jawbreaker and Nightshade were too big to fit into Hashtag's van, Bumblebee and the Terrans attached a horse trailer they found in the barn to Hashtag's bumper. Once the trailer was secured, Nightshade, Jawbreaker, Twitch, and Thrash climbed in. Robby and Mo jumped into Bumblebee's interior. They would ride to the races in style!

CHAPTER 3
A MYSTERIOUS YELLOW CAR

Sitting beside his wife, Dot, on the crowded grandstand at the speedway, Alex Malto lowered his binoculars. "What a treat!" he said, smiling. "You sure fooled me when you said you were bringing me to the Witwicky Botanical Gardens!"

"I know how much you love motor sports," Dot said, "so when I learned about the races, I decided to surprise you."

"You're the greatest, Dot," Alex said. He returned his attention to the speedway's two oval racetracks, which were separated by a tall observation tower. Sports cars zoomed around one track while motorbikes zoomed around the other. Flying overhead, several camera drones recorded all the action.

Alex Malto was a history professor and an expert on Transformers robots. Dot Malto was a veteran of the Transformers War and was friends with Megatron and Optimus Prime. Although the Witwicky

National Park employed Dot as a park ranger, she had a second job as a top-secret agent for G.H.O.S.T.

Alex leaned close to Dot and whispered, "Agent Schloder sure can be annoying, but it was nice of him to let you have the day off."

"To tell the truth," Dot said, "I'm working right now! Schloder assigned me and a few dozen other G.H.O.S.T. agents to come here and to keep our eyes open for vehicles that might be robots in disguise."

Alex sighed. "A minute ago, I was wishing Bumblebee and the kids could have somehow been here watching the races with us. Now I'm relieved they're at home!"

"We can't let them be seen in public," Dot said. "If G.H.O.S.T. learns about the existence of the Terrans and that Bumblebee is living with us on the farm, G.H.O.S.T. would take them away from us!"

Alex sighed. "Let's hope the Terrans and Bumblebee will soon be free to go wherever they want." He peered through his binoculars again. When he saw two tall, familiar bots move into view near the base of the speedway's observation tower, he said, "Dot, were you expecting to see Optimus Prime and Megatron here?"

"What?" Dot reached for the binoculars. She looked at her two friends as they watched the racing vehicles. She handed the binoculars back to Alex and said, "Sit tight. I'll be right back."

Leaving her seat, Dot moved through the crowd and down and across the grandstand, making her way to the observation tower. When she arrived before Optimus Prime and Megatron, they looked down at her with surprise.

"Don't tell me," Dot said. "Agent Schloder ordered you to come here too."

"That is correct, Dot," Optimus Prime said.

Megatron scanned the crowd and said, "Dorothy, I've spotted fifty-six undercover G.H.O.S.T. agents. Why did Schloder send so many?"

"To get the job done!" Agent Schloder said, surprising the others as he stepped out of a doorway at the base of the observation tower. Holding his own binoculars, Schloder said, "I saw a yellow car entering the parking lot, and I'm certain it's Bumblebee. Let's find him!"

CHAPTER 4
READY, SET, HIDE!

Driving past rows of parked cars, Bumblebee in his alt mode led Hashtag's news van through the speedway's parking lot. They came to a stop side by side in an area that overlooked the motorcycle racetrack and rolled down their windows and opened the trailer door so everyone could talk with one another.

Because Twitch's alt mode was an aerial drone, she immediately took interest in the camera drones swooping above the racetracks. "Wow," she said, "look at those drones move!"

"How about the motorbikes?" asked Mo. "They're going crazy fast!"

Thrash said, "I bet I can go faster than any of them!" Moving past Jawbreaker, Twitch, and Nightshade, Thrash jumped to the ground and rapidly changed into his motorcycle alt mode.

"Thrash! We only came here to *watch* the races, remember?"

Bumblebee scolded. "Now get back inside before someone sees you!"

"Aw, what a party pooper," Thrash said as he returned to the trailer and changed into his bot mode.

Twitch noticed a turquoise minivan parked nearby. "Robby, look over there," she said. "Isn't that Mom and Dad's van?"

Robby gasped. "It is!" he said. "But . . . what's it doing here? They said they were going to the botanical gardens!"

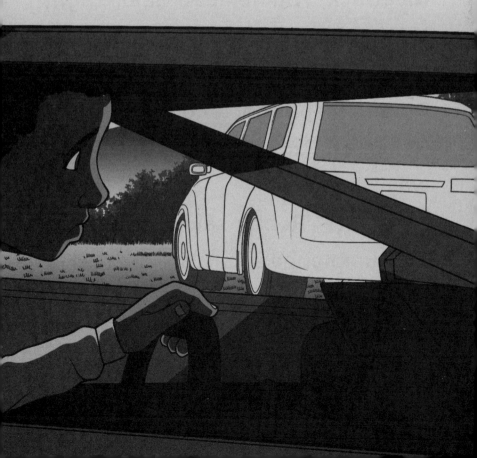

"Uh-oh," Bumblebee said as he adjusted his binocular vision. "I just spotted your mom."

"Where?" Robby and Twitch said at the same time.

"On the other side of the racetrack," Bumblebee said, "right by the observation tower. See her? She's standing next to Optimus Prime, Megatron, and . . . Agent Schloder! And they're walking this way!"

"What?" Robby said. He got out of Bumblebee's car so he had a better view of the area. "Are any other G.H.O.S.T. agents with them?"

"Let me check!" Hashtag said as she activated her built-in radio. "I'm hearing chatter. Sounds like there's G.H.O.S.T. agents all over the place, and they just closed off the exits to the parking lot!"

Mo rushed to the horse trailer door and said, "Robby, get in!" As Robby and Mo squeezed in next to the Terrans, they became suddenly worried about their situation, and soon the Cybertronian Cyber-Sleeves on their arms began to glow. Because the Cyber-Sleeves allowed them to share thoughts and feelings with the Terrans, the Terrans' eyes began to glow with worry too.

"In hindsight, I believe we should have remained at home today," said Nightshade.

"Where's Dad? Maybe he could help us?" asked Jawbreaker.

"Maybe you're right!" Mo said.
"Twitch, can you find Dad?"

"I'm on it!" Twitch said. As she scrambled out of the trailer, Bumblebee told her to be careful and rolled up his windows. Twitch changed into her drone mode and flew away so swiftly that no one saw her leave the trailer and rise over the speedway.

Hashtag and all her hidden
passengers stayed very quiet as
Optimus Prime, Megatron, Dot, and
Agent Schloder walked up beside
Bumblebee. Schloder said, "Show
yourself, Bumblebee! We've got you
surrounded!"

CHAPTER 5
SAFE AT THE FINISH

As vehicles continued to race around the tracks at the speedway, G.H.O.S.T. agents moved across the parking lot toward the yellow sports car.

Megatron, Optimus Prime, and Dot recognized the news van parked next to Bumblebee, and they knew the van was really Hashtag. Hoping to distract Schloder and the other agents, Dot faced Bumblebee's alt mode and said, "This looks like a common sports car to me. My husband has one just like it."

Before Schloder could respond, a distant voice called out, "Hey! Why are you surrounding my car?!"

Everyone turned to see Alex Malto running toward them. He was almost out of breath when he stopped beside his wife and said, "What's going on? Did someone damage my car? I just had it waxed!"

"This is your car?" Schloder said.

"Of course it is!" Alex said. "If it weren't mine, could I do this?" He pulled a set of keys from his pocket, opened the driver's door, seated himself, and started the engine.

Megatron tilted his head slightly and said, "Sounds like you recently had a tune-up, Professor Malto."

Schloder grimaced. He turned to the G.H.O.S.T. agents and said, "False alarm. Open the exits and return to headquarters at once."

Schloder and the agents walked off, returned to their vehicles, and left the parking lot. When they were gone, Bumblebee turned off his own engine, and Alex got out to stand beside Dot. Alex looked up to see a descending drone and said, "Here comes Twitch!"

Twitch landed near the group. "Dad, is everyone okay?" she asked.

"Yes!" Alex said. "Thank goodness you found me in the stands and told me where to find Bumblebee! But why are you kids here at the speedway?"

"That's what I'd like to know," added Dot.

Optimus Prime looked right at Bumblebee. "It's all my fault," Bumblebee admitted. "The kids found out about the races, and . . . well, we just wanted to see the cars and motorcycles."

Dot stepped over to the horse trailer and looked inside. Seeing Mo, Robby, Thrash, Nightshade, and Jawbreaker squeezed inside, she said, "You all know you're supposed to be at home."

"But you're supposed to be at the botanical gardens!" Robby pointed out.

Alex chuckled.

"What's so funny?" Dot asked.

"None of us are where we're supposed to be!" said Alex.

Nightshade turned to their parents. "I anticipate an exhaustive family discussion about the importance of obeying the rules and telling the truth," they said.

"May I suggest you have that discussion some other time?" asked Megatron. "Because right now, I'm curious to see if yellow cars are faster than green cars."

"And so long as we're all here," Optimus Prime added, "we may as well watch the races . . . together."

Dot looked at her children and smiled. "All right, kids," she said. "We'll talk later . . . after the races."

The Malto children cheered, "Yay, Mom!"

Ready for another  adventure?

Here's a sneak peek of Book 2,

THE TERRANS
COOK UP SOME MISCHIEF!

Bumblebee was watching Twitch, Thrash, Hashtag, Nightshade, and Jawbreaker playing tag outside the barn on the Malto family farm when Thrash said, "Everybody freeze!"

All five Terrans stopped suddenly. Bumblebee said, "What's wrong?"

Thrash said, "This game would be more fun if Mo and Robby joined in."

Nightshade said, "I believe they are still partaking in their evening meal."

"It's too bad we don't eat food," Twitch said. "Then we could join them."

"But we're family too," Thrash said. "We should be with them, even if we don't eat!"

"Let's see if they're finished," Hashtag said.